The Easter Bunny Is Missing!

To Jenne and Gina
— S. M.

ISBN-13: 978-0-439-92959-2
ISBN-10: 0-439-92959-8

12 11 10 9 8 7 6 5 4 3 2 7 8 9 10 11 12/0

Printed in the U.S.A.
First printing, March 2007

Book design by Jennifer Rinaldi Windau

The Easter Bunny Is Missing!

by Steve Metzger
Illustrated by Barbara Spurll

SCHOLASTIC INC.
New York Toronto London Auckland Sydney
Mexico City New Delhi Hong Kong Buenos Aires

It was the day before Easter and spring was in the air. The forest animals had gathered at Blueberry Meadow to plan for their annual Easter party, which always took place after the children found their Easter eggs.

"I can't wait for our party!" exclaimed Bear.

"I'll bring the refreshments!" said Fox.

"The Crickets are scheduled to play!" said Frog. "Their music is hoppin'!"

"But, where's the Easter Bunny?" asked Fox, looking around. "He's not here."

"How can we celebrate Easter without the Easter Bunny?" asked Mole nervously. "Who will deliver the Easter eggs?"

"Calm down, everyone," said Turtle. "Maybe he just got lost. Let's try to find him."

Bear and Fox looked behind every tree in the forest.

Mole checked all of the rabbit holes and burrows.

Turtle and Frog searched around the lake.

"Any luck?" asked Turtle. The other animals shook their heads.

"The Easter Bunny is missing," Bear said sadly.

"We've got to do something," added Mole. "The children will be sad if they don't get their Easter eggs tomorrow."

"One of us will just have to fill in for the Easter Bunny this year," said Fox. "It should be me . . . and I'll show you why!"

Carrying a basket of colorful eggs, Fox led his friends out of the forest.

"Watch me!" Fox called out as she put on a pair of bunny ears. "I'd be the fastest Easter Bunny ever!" She took the Easter basket and quickly raced around to the children's homes, hiding eggs under the bushes.

"Wait a minute!" said Mole. "You're too fast! You dropped some of the eggs along the way. Children will find them much too easily. Sorry, Fox, but you can't be the Easter Bunny."

"Let me do it!" yelled Frog. "I'm the best one for the job!"

"And why is that?" asked Bear.

Frog smiled. "You've heard that Easter Bunny song, right? 'Hippity-hoppity, Easter's on its way.' " Frog sang. "Well, who does hippity-hoppity better than me?"

Frog grabbed the Easter basket and went bouncing down the path.

"Hippity-hoppity, hippity-hoppity, Easter's on its way!" Frog sang out. He didn't notice that some of the eggs fell out and broke.

"No way!" said Bear. "With all that bouncing up and down, you'll crack all the eggs."

"I should be the Easter Bunny," said Mole quietly.

Mole found the best hiding spots for the Easter eggs . . . but he couldn't always find his way out.

"Sorry, Mole," said Turtle.

"I'd be the best Easter Bunny because I'm the strongest," said Bear. He loaded up his basket with dozens of eggs.

But as he lumbered down the path, he banged his basket against the trees, crushing many eggs.

"I guess I'm too strong," said Bear forlornly.

"That leaves me," said Turtle. He strapped the basket of eggs to his shell and toddled down the path. But when he finally reached a hiding place, thirty minutes had gone by.

Fox shook her head. "By the time you finish hiding all the eggs, it'll be Christmas."

"I don't care," said Turtle. "I still want to be the Easter Bunny!"

"No!" said Bear. "I want to do it!"

The animals argued back and forth, filling the forest with their shouting voices. The racket got louder and **louder** and **LOUDER!**

"What's going on here!" a familiar voice rang out. "I could hear you all the way down Daffodil Road."

"Easter Bunny!" Frog shouted. "You're here!"

"Where have you been?" asked Bear.

"On vacation," the Easter Bunny replied. "Hawaii was so much fun that I decided to stay a little longer. I hope you weren't worried about me. Now what is all the fighting about?"

"Oh, nothing," replied Mole sheepishly. "Nothing at all."

"It's great to see you!" the Easter Bunny said as he began putting Easter eggs into his basket. "But now it's time for me to get to work. I have lots to do for tomorrow. Hippity-hoppity!"

"And a big hippity-hoppity to you, too," said Frog. "Happy Easter!"

The Easter Bunny skipped off to hide the eggs . . .
and he didn't drop a single one.